VICTORY SCHOOL SUPERSTARS

Sports Illustrated KIDS

STONE ARCH BOOKS
a capstone imprint

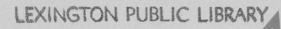

ORY
OOL
STARS

Sports
Illustrated
KID$

Five Fouls
and You're Out!

by Val Priebe
illustrated by Jorge Santillan

STONE ARCH BOOKS
a capstone imprint

Sports Illustrated KIDS *Five Fouls and You're Out!*
is published by Stone Arch Books – A Capstone Imprint
1710 Roe Crest Drive
North Mankato, Minnesota 56003
www.capstonepub.com

Art Director and Designer: Bob Lentz
Creative Director: Heather Kindseth
Production Specialist: Michelle Biedscheid

Timeline photo credits: Library of Congress (top);
Sports Illustrated/Bob Rosato (bottom right), John W.
McDonough (bottom left), Robert Beck (middle left),
Walter Iooss Jr. (middle right).

Library of Congress Cataloging-in-Publication Data is
available on the Library of Congress website.

ISBN: 978-1-4342-2228-2 (library binding)
ISBN: 978-1-4342-3075-1 (paperback)

Summary: Carmen must learn to stop fouling out of her
basketball games.

Printed in the United States of America in Stevens Point, Wisconsin.
052015   008959R

TABLE of CONTENTS

CHAPTER 1
Out of the Game.................. 6

CHAPTER 2
Foul Talk 16

CHAPTER 3
Practice Time 22

CHAPTER 4
Friends to the Rescue 26

CHAPTER 5
Figuring It Out 36

CHAPTER 6
Move Your Feet................... 44

CARMEN SKORE

Basketball

AGE: 10

GRADE: 4

SUPER SPORTS ABILITY: Super dribbling

VICTORY SCHOOL SUPERSTARS

CARMEN   ALICIA   JOSH   DANNY   KENZIE   TYLER

VICTORY SCHOOL MAP

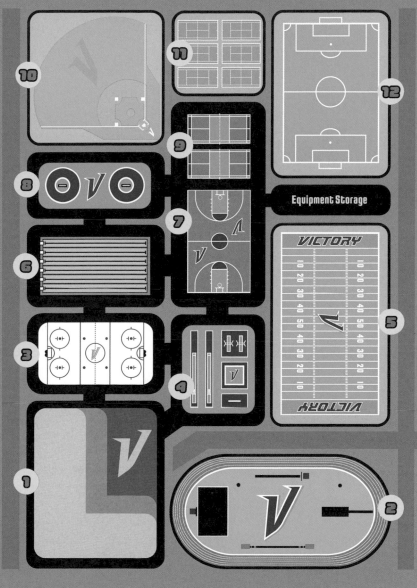

Equipment Storage

VICTORY

1. Main Offices/Classrooms
2. Track and Field
3. Hockey/Figure Skating
4. Gymnastics
5. Football
6. Swimming
7. Basketball
8. Wrestling
9. Volleyball
10. Baseball/Softball
11. Tennis
12. Soccer

Out of the Game

I bounce the basketball off my elbow. It hits my right hand and rolls up my arm, across my shoulders, and down my left arm. I spin the ball on my pointer finger. Then I pass it behind my back to one of my teammates.

She shoots and scores! Now my Victory School basketball team needs to play defense.

Coach Holland yells at me from the sidelines. "Play smart, Carmen!"

I guard the point guard for the other team. I am not really thinking about it. My hands just reach out for the ball. But I hit the girl's arm instead. That's a foul for sure.

TWEEEET! The referee blows her whistle. "Foul on number nine!" she yells.

My stomach drops. I wait for what I know the referee will say next.

"That is five fouls, nine. You are out of the game," she says to me. Every player is allowed four fouls in a game of basketball. If a player gets foul number five, they can't play for the rest of the game.

As I take a seat on the bench, Coach Holland is talking to Sadie, the other point guard for Victory. Sadie's super skill is passing. No matter what, Sadie can always get the ball to her teammates.

With my perfect dribbling skills, I am Victory's number-one point guard. But I'm no help to my team when I foul out of the game. Thank goodness for Sadie.

There are still five minutes left in the game. Five minutes is a long time in basketball. Victory has a small lead. I am really letting my team down by fouling out.

In the end, we win, but I was worried until the clock ran out of time.

Before heading to the locker room, I stop to talk to Coach Holland. "Coach, I am really sorry that I fouled out again. I don't know what's wrong!"

I'm telling the truth. I have been getting five fouls a lot in the last couple of weeks, and I don't know why.

Last week, we lost a game after I fouled out.

"I don't know what's wrong either," says Coach Holland. "We really need to figure it out, though. Your team needs you."

I feel awful. I know that Coach Holland is right.

"I'll think about it," I tell Coach. In fact, I doubt I will think about anything else tonight. As I walk into the locker room, I spot Sadie.

"Good game, Sadie!" I tell her. And I really mean it. Sadie saved the game. "Thanks, Carmen, but you are the super dribbler," says Sadie, smiling.

"Yeah," I agree. "But I fouled out again. You kept us in and won the game."

Sadie just smiles and shakes her head. "Just quit fouling, Carmen!" she says, laughing.

I make myself smile, but inside I am upset. It's not like I'm trying to foul out.

It's the day after the game. I am sitting at lunch with my friends Tyler, Josh, and Lynsey.

Tyler plays basketball, too. His super skill is shooting. While we eat, Tyler shoots used napkins into the trash can on the other side of the lunchroom. He never misses, and he doesn't even look!

Lynsey plays soccer. Josh is a super skater. As we eat lunch, I dribble my basketball on the floor next to me.

"So Carmen," says Tyler, "we were all at your game yesterday. Fouled out again, huh? What's up with that?"

"I don't know!" I say. "I don't do it on purpose! I mean, it's no fun to foul out. I need to figure it out!"

"It's okay, Carmen. We know you don't do it on purpose," Lynsey says. "We'll help you figure it out."

Josh chimes in. "Have you tried watching games on TV?" he asks. "My dad says you can learn a lot from watching really good players."

I sigh. "My dad thinks we don't need a TV," I remind him. "So I can't watch any basketball."

Josh says, "Maybe Tyler and I should come to your practice today." Lynsey is already shaking her head. She knows about Coach Holland's rules.

"Thanks, Josh, but Coach Holland doesn't let other students into practice," I say. "She says they break our focus."

"We'll think of something," Tyler says. Josh and Lynsey agree. I am so lucky to have such great friends!

CHAPTER 3

Practice Time

At the end of practice, Coach Holland has us scrimmage against each other. A scrimmage is like a real game, but we don't keep score. When Coach Holland blows her whistle, we are all tired and sweaty.

"Good work today, girls!" says Coach. "Have a really great weekend, and be ready for Monday's game!"

"Superstars!" we all yell together. I start to jog to the locker room, but Coach calls me back.

"Carmen," she says. "I was watching you play today."

I feel confused. She's the coach. She watches everyone.

Coach says, "Your dribbling was perfect, as usual. But I was trying to find out why you are fouling out."

I nod, as my face turns red with shame.

Coach seems to know what I am thinking. "Don't worry, Carmen," she says. "We'll figure it out. Spend some time this weekend thinking about it, okay?"

"Okay, Coach," I say. Coach smiles. I run as fast as I can to the locker room to change. I know my dad is waiting in front of the school for me. Right now, I really wish my super skill was defense.

Friends to the Rescue

I sit at dinner that night wishing we had a TV so that I could watch basketball like Josh said. Most of the time, I don't mind not having a TV, but I think it would be helpful now. It's no good talking to my dad about it, though.

I am thinking so hard about fouls that I don't know the phone rang until my dad hands it to me.

"It's Lynsey," Dad says.

"Hi, Lynsey!" I say, waving my dad away. "What's up?"

"Well," says Lynsey, "I was wondering if you wanted to sleep over tonight."

I smile. I don't think I have smiled all
day. That is not like me at all!

"I have to ask my dad," I say. "Can I
call you back?" After I hang up, I race to
the kitchen. Dad agrees to the sleepover,
and I call Lynsey right back.

Almost before I can pack my bag, I hear,
"HOOONNNNKKK!"

Lynsey's mom's car is in the driveway, and Lynsey is leaning over to honk the horn.

"Have fun, honey," says Dad. He gives me a hug good-bye. "See you tomorrow!"

Lynsey is talking as soon as I open the car door.

"Guess what, Carmen!" she exclaims. "We're going ice skating!"

"Ice skating?" I ask. I am totally confused.

"Yep!" says Lynsey. "Tyler and Josh figured it out."

What is she talking about?

Lynsey looks at my face and laughs. "Sorry, Carmen!" she says. "I am just so excited!"

I start to get a little mad at Lynsey. "What are you excited about?" I ask.

"I'll tell you when we get to the rink," says Lynsey. "It will all make more sense there."

Thankfully, we are at the ice center in just a few minutes. I can't wait any longer! Lynsey finally starts explaining.

"Josh and Tyler watched some basketball on TV, since you can't. They had Tyler's dad watch, too. They figured out why you keep fouling out!" Lynsey explains.

My heart does a flip-flop in my chest. "Why?" I ask. But before she can answer, I notice the guys.

Tyler is waiting for us on the ice. But Josh is in the middle of the rink spinning on one skate. He is spinning so fast that he is just a blur of his red coat, blue jeans, and black cap.

Without slowing down at all, he stops, skates forward a few feet, jumps, and twirls in the air at least four times. Then he lands on one skate. Just like it's nothing, Josh floats across the ice toward Lynsey and me. My mouth is hanging open.

"Here," he says, breathing hard. "These are my sister's skates. They should fit you. Let's get to work!"

CHAPTER 5

Figuring It Out

"How is skating going to help me play better defense?" I ask.

"It is really simple," says Tyler. He looks proud of himself. "We were watching basketball with my dad. He pointed out that all of the really good players do not try to steal the ball."

I nod. This is true.

Josh says, "The good ones just move their feet and stay between the person with the basketball and the basket. They just wait for the other player to make a mistake!"

I start to see what Josh and Tyler are talking about.

"So," says Tyler, "we know that your super skill is dribbling. You always want to have the ball in your hands, right?"

I nod my head at Tyler again. Of course I always want to have the ball in my hands!

Josh keeps talking. "The players that aren't so good just reach in and try to steal the ball."

Josh is right. I always just try to steal the ball. I don't move my feet.

I finally know what I'm doing wrong, but I am still confused. "Thanks for figuring that out, guys! But I still don't get why we are skating," I say.

"Because you can only use your feet for skating, Carmen!" exclaims Josh. "You can't use your hands!"

Josh is very excited about teaching me to skate. I put on the skates and carefully make my way to the ice.

Josh gives me some skating pointers. I practice moving backward while I play defense on Tyler. I fall down a lot. But I need to play good defense, so I keep getting up and trying again.

Practice is the only thing that will make me better. And Lynsey, Josh, and Tyler are really helpful. I just hope it will help in Monday's game!

Move Your Feet

Move your feet, I think to myself over and over. I move my feet and wait for the Springfield point guard to make a mistake. She is very good, but she does not have my super skill.

Finally, she dribbles the ball just a little bit too high. I reach out and steal the ball. I dribble down the court, shoot, and score.

TWEEEEET! The referee blows the whistle. But this time it is because the Springfield coach has called a time-out.

The Victory fans are cheering so loud that it is hard to hear Coach Holland. There are just four minutes left in the game. I have three fouls, and Victory is winning by three points.

Coach Holland is yelling over the noise, "Just keep playing good defense. No fouls!"

Three minutes left. We make another basket.

Two minutes left. Springfield makes two baskets in a row. Now we are only winning by one point! *Move your feet!* I tell myself again.

One minute left. The girl I'm guarding has the ball again. If I can steal it again — without fouling — we might be able to score. And that would seal the win!

I spot my chance. My feet move into position, and I steal the ball with ease.

I look for open teammates as I dribble toward our basket. Jill, our tallest girl, is open under the basket, so I pass to her.

Jill shoots, but misses. But then she gets her own rebound and scores. That's Jill's super skill, rebounding. The Victory fans yell really loud as the clock reads 0:00. We win!

I know that I still have a lot of practicing to do, but my friends are right. Knowing the problem sure does help you fix it!

GLOSSARY

confused (kuhn-FYOOZD)—did not understand

defense (DEE-fens)—the team that does not have control of the ball

dribbling (DRIB-uhl-ing)—in basketball, bouncing the ball while running, keeping it under control

foul (FOUL)—an action in sports that is against the rules

point guard (POINT GARD)—the player that controls the ball and calls the plays

rebound (REE-bound)—to get control of the ball after a missed shot

scrimmage (SKRIM-ij)—a game played for practice

time-out (TIME-OUT)—a short break during a game

ABOUT THE AUTHOR

Val Priebe lives in St. Paul, Minnesota, with four dogs, a cat named Cowboy, and a guy named Nick. Besides writing books, she loves to spend her time reading, knitting, cooking, and coaching basketball. Val is also the author of *It's Hard to Dribble with Your Feet*, another book about Carmen in the Victory School Superstars series.

ABOUT THE ILLUSTRATOR

Jorge Santillan got his start illustrating in the children's sections of local newspapers. He opened his own illustration studio in 2005. His creative team specializes in books, comics, and children magazines. Jorge lives in Mendoza, Argentina, with his wife, Bety; son, Luca; and their four dogs, Fito, Caro, Angie, and Sammy.

BASKETBALL IN HISTORY

 1891 Dr. James Naismith invents basketball.

 1892 Senda Berenson adapts the rules for women, who play in **long skirts.**

 1926 The first national women's basketball championship is held.

 1976 Women's basketball becomes an **Olympic sport.**

 1978 The Women's Professional Basketball League is formed with eight teams. The league plays just three seasons.

 1984 West Virginia's Georgeann Wells becomes the first female college player to make a dunk during a game.

 1986 Nancy Lieberman joins the Springfield Fame, a professional men's team in the United States Basketball League.

 1997 The **Women's National Basketball Association (WNBA)** is formed.

 2002 **Lisa Leslie** makes the first dunk ever in a WNBA game.

 2008 The United States wins its fourth straight **Olympic gold medal** in women's basketball.

VICTORY SCHOOL SUPERSTARS

Five Fouls and You're Out!

It's a Wrestling Mat, Not a Dance Floor

There's a Hurricane in the Pool!

There's No Crying in Baseball

Who Wants to Play Just for Kicks?

You Can't Spike Your Serves

Read them ALL!

STONE ARCH BOOKS
a capstone imprint